The
Railway
Rabbits

Bramble and the Treasure Hunt

Georgie Adams
Illustrated by Anna Currey

Orion
Children's Books

First published in Great Britain in 2012
by Orion Children's Books
a division of the Orion Publishing Group Ltd
Orion House
5 Upper St Martin's Lane
London WC2H 9EA
An Hachette Livre UK Company

1 3 5 7 9 10 8 6 4 2

The Orion Publishing Group's policy is to use papers that are natural,
renewable and recyclable products and made from wood grown in
sustainable forests. The logging and manufacturing processes are
expected to conform to the environmental regulations of the country
of origin.

A catalogue record for this book is available from the British Library.

ISBN 978 1 4440 0254 6

www.orionbooks.co.uk
www.georgieadams.com

For Tom
With love – G.A.

The Ripple River Valley

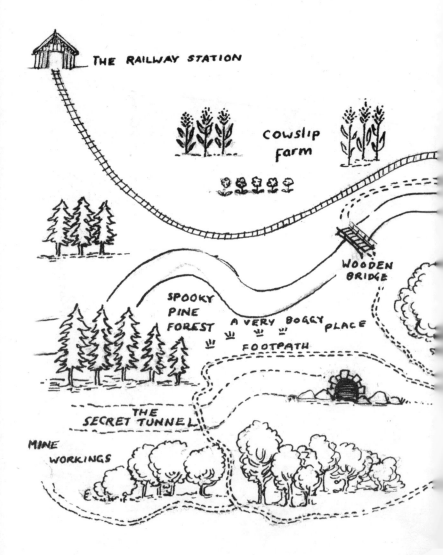

THE RAILWAY STATION

COWSLIP FARM

WOODEN BRIDGE

SPOOKY PINE FOREST

A VERY BOGGY PLACE

FOOTPATH

THE SECRET TUNNEL

MINE WORKINGS

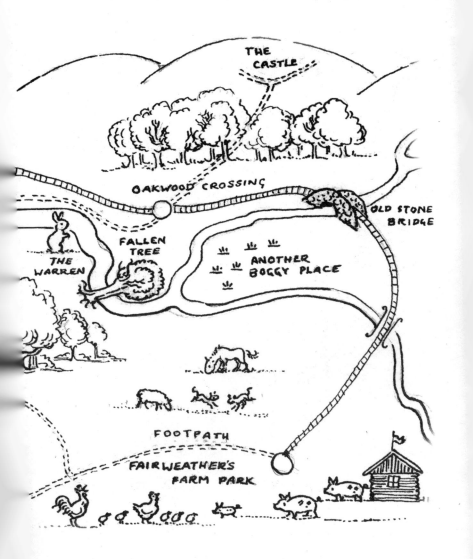

THE CASTLE

OAKWOOD CROSSING

OLD STONE BRIDGE

FALLEN TREE

THE WARREN

ANOTHER BOGGY PLACE

FOOTPATH

FAIRWEATHER'S FARM PARK

The Greybacks are Coming!

1

On a morning in autumn, Barley and Mellow Longears and the five young Longears rabbits, Bramble, Bracken, Berry, Fern and Wisher, were up earlier than usual. Some friends were coming and everyone was very excited – all except Barley who had never met them. Meeting new rabbits always made Barley nervous. He paced up and down outside the burrow.

"Please, tell me their names again,"
he said to Mellow. "I know you've told me
before. But I keep forgetting!"

"Lop and Lilly Greyback," said Mellow.
"And their twins, Tansy and Teasel."

"Tansy and Teasel are fun!"
said Bramble.

"And naughty," said Bracken.

"They took us to their secret place on
River Island once," said Berry.

"Where we got stuck," Fern reminded
them.

"And had to be rescued," said Wisher.

"By ME!" said Mellow.

"I remember," said Barley. "It was the
day you all went to Burrow Bank. How
could I forget?"

"If it hadn't been for Marr," said Fern.
"We could have been there for EVER!"

"Hm!" said Barley, tugging his ear. "I can see I shall have to keep my eye on Tansy and Teasel. They sound like trouble."

Just then, Blinker Badger came along.

"Trouble?" said Blinker. "What trouble, my dear old friend? It's a fine day. A little misty, it's true, but it will clear when the sun comes out. And the hedgerow is full of nuts and blackberries! So what's wrong, Barley Longears?"

Barley explained about their visitors.

"Those twins will be up to mischief, I know it," he said.

"I'm sure everything will be fine, Barley," said Mellow. "Lop and Lilly will make sure Tansy and Teasel behave."

"I hope you're right!" said Barley.

Mellow went to tidy the burrow, leaving Barley and Blinker to talk. Bramble, Bracken, Berry, Fern and Wisher couldn't wait for the Greybacks to arrive.

"Let's go down to the wooden bridge," said Bramble. "They'll cross the river there. It's the quickest way from Burrow Bank."

"Good idea," said Bracken.

"Race you," said Berry.

"Wait for us," said Fern and Wisher.

"Stay together!" said Barley. "You must be extra careful this morning. A fox, or Burdock could sneak up on you in the mist."

"We will!" they said.

Barley and Blinker watched them dash towards the River Ripple.

Barley sighed.

"I can't help worrying about them,"
he said.

Blinker nodded.

"I understand," he said. "I feel the
same about my cubs. I left them playing
in Oak Wood. They are with their mother
and I'm sure they're all right, but . . ."

"What?" said Barley.

"Well, lately I've heard stories about a strange beast," said Blinker. "He has big yellow eyes at the front and red ones behind. Just think! An animal that looks both ways at once must be very dangerous!"

Barley nearly jumped out of his skin.

"A beast with four eyes!" he cried. "Where?"

"I don't know if it's true," said Blinker. "You know how these stories get about. But some say they've seen the creature racing across Windy Moor at night, and part of it lies close to Oak Wood. The beast moves so fast he can be anywhere in the blink of an eye.

I'd defend my family with tooth and claw, but I still worry about them. Now, I must be off. Goodbye!"

"Oh, buttercups!" said Barley. "As if I didn't have enough to worry about today. I must warn everyone to watch out for a beast!"

Bramble, Bracken, Berry, Fern and Wisher waited at the little wooden bridge for their friends to arrive. For a while they played Hop-Back. Then they chased each other over the bridge and back again. When there was still no sign of the Greybacks, Bramble began to get restless.

"Where are they?" he said. "We've been waiting for such a long time."

"Maybe they got lost?" said Bracken.

"Maybe they're hiding from Burdock?" said Berry.

"I hope they're okay," said Fern. "Wisher, what do you think?"

Wisher was gazing down at the river. The River Ripple swished and swirled under the bridge in its Not-Such-A-Hurry way.

She'd been half-listening and had a faraway look in her eyes.

Her ears were tingling too – a sign that soon there might be danger – and she heard a voice inside her head:

High on a hill where the wind blows cold,
There stands a rock, many full moons old.

Wisher wondered what it could mean.

"What do I think about what?" she said.

"Wisher!" cried the others.

They were used to her funny ways, but sometimes they lost patience.

"We were talking about Tansy and Teasel," said Fern. "They should have been here by now."

"Oh," said Wisher. "Maybe the message was a clue?"

"Message?" said Bramble.

"Yes," said Wisher. "Something about a rock . . ."

Just then, Barley came hurrying over.

"Back to the burrow!" he said. "There's a beast! Blinker says it's big. It has four eyes!"

The young rabbits gasped.

"Oooo!" said Fern. "What if the beast has caught Tansy and Teasel? We'll never see them again, EVER!"

Barley tried to calm her down.

"We don't know anything has happened to anybody," he said. "I'm sure your friends will be here soon. Let's go home and wait for them there."

"Are you sure this is the right way?" said Lop to Lilly. He peered through the mist, trying to see where they were.

"I *think* so," said Lilly. "Mellow and Barley live up-river. If we follow the riverbank it should take us there."

Lop and Lilly, Tansy and Teasel
hopped along a winding pathway
through the trees. At last, they came to
a grassy bank, which sloped steeply
downwards. They couldn't see to the
bottom, because a few wisps of white
were still swirling about.

"Is this the riverbank?" said Lop.

"I can't hear the river," said Lilly.

"I can't hear anything," said Tansy.

"Spooky!" said Teasel.

"Let's go down and see," said Lop.

Tansy and Teasel gave each other a cheeky grin. Each knew *exactly* what the other was thinking!

Before Lop or Lilly could stop them, Tansy and Teasel rolled down the bank. Over and over, faster and faster, until . . .

Thump!

Bump!

They landed on stones, packed between iron rails.

"Ouch!" said Tansy.

"Ow!" said Teasel.

"You silly rabbits!" said Lop, running towards them. "These are the Red Dragon's tracks!"

"Sorry, Parr," said Tansy and Teasel.

Then they all felt the ground tremble, and heard the shriek of a whistle.

Whooo-Wheeep!

The four Greybacks leapt from the tracks over to the bank on the far side. A moment later, the Red Dragon came thundering down the line, spitting sparks and belching clouds of sooty black smoke.

Clickerty-clack. Clickerty-click!

It rattled and clattered its way along the valley, then disappeared round a bend.

"Phew!" said Tansy.

"That was close," said Teasel.

"Which way now?" said Lop, brushing smuts from his fur. "We don't want to cross the tracks again."

"We'll climb the bank," said Lilly. "We should see more from up there."

But when they got to the top of the bank, they were all very surprised. It was a very wild and bleak place.

"There aren't many trees," said Tansy.

"Or bushes," said Teasel.

"That's because it's a moor," said Lop.

Tansy spotted a hill. There was a big rock at the top.

"That rock looks just like a rabbit!" she said.

"You're right," said Lilly. "How strange!"

"Never mind the rock," said Lop. "There's a wood just beyond the hill. We'll be safer there. Who knows what terrible creatures live on the moor. Let's go!"

Rowan's Rock
2

Blinker Badger hurried on his way home to Oak Wood. He took his usual path down to the river and along a tree, which had fallen across the water. Then it was only a short run to Oakwood Crossing and the tunnel. Whenever Blinker went through the tunnel he thought about the people-folk who'd made it.

"They must have known I use this path from the wood to the river over and over again. Just like my father, and *his* father before him. It used to be dangerous crossing the Red Dragon's tracks, but not any more. The tunnel goes under the tracks. And it's just the right size for a badger like me. Clever people-folk!"

Blinker ran through the tunnel and out the other side. He was just entering Oak Wood when he saw a family of rabbits. He knew most animals living in the wood, but these rabbits were strangers.

The two young rabbits looked exactly the same. They had soft, grey coats with white tummies and paws – except one had floppy ears. When they saw Blinker, they scampered over.

"Hello," said the one who didn't have floppy ears. "I'm Tansy Greyback, and this is my brother Teasel. We're looking for our friends, Bramble, Bracken, Berry, Fern and Wisher Longears, and we've been going round and round in circles for ages and . . ."

"We're completely lost," said Teasel. "Sorry about my sister. She never stops talking!"

"I was only telling him the facts," said Tansy. Then to Blinker: "Could you help us, please?"

29

"I'd be delighted to help any friends of the Longears family," said Blinker. "They are my friends too. I've just come from their burrow. They're looking forward to seeing you. I'm Blinker Badger, by the way."

Just then, Lop and Lilly joined them.

"This is Blinker Badger," said Tansy. "And these are my parents, Lop and Lilly Greyback."

"They're my parents as well,"
said Teasel.

"Obviously," said Tansy, rolling
her eyes.

"Welcome to Oak Wood!" said
Blinker.

"Thank you," said Lilly. "I'm afraid we took a wrong path."

"Quite a few wrong ones!" said Lop. "We've just come from the moor."

Blinker gasped.

"You . . . you came by Windy Moor?" he said.

"Yes," said Lilly.

"But we didn't know its name," said Lop.

"We saw a hill with a rabbit on top," said Tansy.

"It wasn't a real one," said Teasel. "It was just a rock that looked like a rabbit."

"I was about to *say*," said Tansy.

"You must have passed Rowan's Rock," said Blinker. "There's a legend about it." He paused, trying to find the right words without causing alarm.

"Er, you didn't happen to notice a large animal . . . a wild creature . . . a *beast*, did you?"

"A b-b-beast!" said Tansy and Teasel.

Lop and Lilly shook their heads.

"I said there'd be terrible things on the moor," said Lop.

"Well, we've had two lucky escapes this morning," said Lilly. "First, the Red Dragon. Now the beast!"

Tansy tried not to think of monsters. She remembered something else Blinker had said, which sounded interesting.

"Please, Blinker Badger," she said. "What is the legend of Rowan's Rock?"

"We don't have time for stories," said Lilly. "Barley and Mellow will be wondering where we are."

"Quite right," said Blinker. "Anyway, I'm sure Mellow knows the tale. Most rabbits do. Ask her."

After telling Lop and Lilly how to find the Longears' burrow, Blinker continued on his way.

"They're here!" cried Bramble. "I saw them first."

He ran across the grass to greet them with Bracken, Berry, Fern and Wisher.

"Tansy! Teasel!" they all said excitedly.

"Great to see you," said Tansy.

"Yeah," said Teasel. "We've got lots to tell you."

"Lilly! Lop!" said Mellow, hugging them both at once. "We thought you were never coming. Barley. Barley? Where are you? Come and meet everyone."

Barley had been sitting on his tree stump keeping watch for Burdock and the four-eyed beast. He'd been concentrating so hard he hadn't noticed the Greybacks arrive. When he heard Mellow calling he hurried over.

"Hello," he said, a little shyly. He shook Lop's paw and smiled at Lilly. "Welcome to our burrow!"

Then to the twins: "Ah, you must
be Tansy and Teasel. I've heard about
you two."

Tansy and Teasel grinned at Barley.
He thought they looked a mischievous
pair!

"I hope you've heard good things,"
said Lilly. She knew her naughty twins
too well.

"Oh, er, yes," said Barley.

Mellow came to his rescue.

"You must stay the night," she said
to Lop and Lilly. "You've had a long

journey and we have so much to talk about! Our burrow is a small but I'm sure we can find enough room."

"Hooray!" cried Bramble, Bracken, Berry, Fern and Wisher. They took Tansy and Teasel by the paws and danced around.

"We're going to have such fun!" they sang.

"Come on," said Bramble. "We'll show you around."

At sunset, everyone gathered outside for a feast. Mellow had provided lots of delicious things to eat, which she'd picked from nearby fields and the hedgerow.

They ate:

hazelnuts,

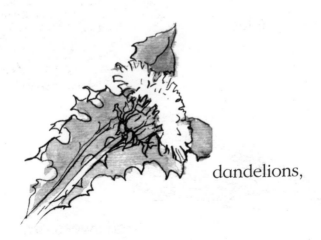

dandelions,

blackberries,

chestnuts,

cabbage leaves,

and sweetcorn.

When their tummies were full, Bramble, Bracken, Berry, Fern, Wisher, Tansy and Teasel lazed around. The grown-ups talked on and on, although Barley kept a look-out for danger.

"You can't be too careful," he said to Lop. "Burdock the buzzard must be hunting somewhere else today. But there's that beast to worry about. It's enormous and has a shiny black coat. It's noisy too. You can hear it roar as it goes along. And it has eyes in the back of its head!"

Lop looked alarmed. The beast sounded much worse than Blinker had said.

"You won't catch me on the moor again," said Lop.

"Yes," said Lilly. "We made a big mistake."

"Let's talk about something else," said Mellow.

Tansy suddenly remembered what she'd been meaning to ask Mellow ever since they'd arrived. She said politely:

"Do you know the legend of Rowan's Rock?"

"Why, yes!" said Mellow. "My mother told me the story when I was a young rabbit." She paused. "Oh dear! I'm afraid it's about a beast!"

"I love stories," said Tansy.

"Scary ones are best!" said Berry.

"Go on, Marr," said Bramble. *"Please!"*

"All right," said Mellow. "But don't blame me if you can't sleep tonight!"

Everyone gathered round and Mellow began:

There was once a brave mother rabbit called Rowan. She lived on a hill with her family, in a burrow beneath a rock. Rowan did her best to keep her young rabbits from harm. She was always on the look-out for buzzards and foxes, and her good friend, the wind, helped too. When the wind blew the scent of enemies to her nose, Rowan would thump the ground. It was the signal for her young ones to hide.

One night, the wind brought a strange smell. Rowan knew the scent of most animals, but this one was different. It wasn't a fox. It wasn't a wolf. This creature was bigger. Much bigger! Suddenly by the light of the moon, Rowan saw a great, hairy beast. And it was coming her way!

Rowan was scared, but she gave the signal. Thump! Thump! Thump! At once, her five young rabbits dived for the burrow. Rowan stood guard, until they were all safe inside. Then she turned and ran. Rowan was quick, but the beast was quicker. With a snap of its terrible jaws, Rowan was no more. "I'll be back," said the beast, licking his lips. "I'll have rabbit again tomorrow!"

The wind saw and heard everything. He was sad about Rowan, and afraid for her children. There was no one to protect them now. The wind told a passing cloud and, before long, they had an idea. Early next morning, the wind blew hard against the big rock, and the cloud poured with rain.

ALL DAY THEY WORKED — THE WIND AND THE RAIN — AND SLOWLY, THE ROCK BEGAN TO CHANGE SHAPE. BY EVENING, THE JOB WAS DONE.

THAT NIGHT THERE WAS A FULL MOON. SURE ENOUGH, THE BEAST RETURNED, BUT THIS TIME HE GOT A SURPRISE. SITTING ON TOP OF THE HILL WAS THE BIGGEST RABBIT HE'D EVER SEEN! THE GIANT RABBIT LOOKED DOWN AT HIM WITH EYES AS BRIGHT AS MOONBEAMS. IT DAZZLED THE BEAST. "I'M OFF!" HE CRIED. THE BEAST RAN AWAY AS FAST AS HE COULD AND WAS NEVER SEEN AGAIN.

"Ever since then the rock has been known as Rowan's Rock," said Mellow. "Some say on windy nights, or whenever there is a full moon, Rowan's ghost appears on the hill."

"Ooo!" said the young rabbits.

"Rowan was very brave," said Bramble. "I loved that story, Marr."

Wisher felt her ears tingle again. This time the voice inside her head seemed to make more sense. She thought the message must have something to do with the legend.

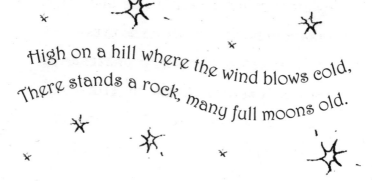

High on a hill where the wind blows cold,
There stands a rock, many full moons old.

Before she could mention it to anyone, Mellow spoke again.

"There's another thing," she said. "Many rabbits believe it's lucky to see Rowan's ghost. Any rabbit brave enough to follow her will find treasure. There's a rhyme about it:

> *One, two, three,*
> *Touch the rock and see,*
> *The ghost of rabbit Rowan,*
> *And a golden apple tree!"*

"Golden apples!" said Bramble excitedly. "Where?"

"I don't know, Bramble," said Mellow. "It's just a story. Besides, I've never yet met a rabbit who has seen Rowan's ghost. Or found a golden apple tree. Now, everybody, time for bed!"

Return to Windy Moor!

3

The Longears' burrow was filled with lively chatter as Mellow tried to find places for her guests to sleep.

"Tansy can share with Fern and me, Marr," said Wisher.

"Good," said Mellow.

"We'll snuggle up together," said Fern.

"And tell scary stories!" said Tansy.

"Teasel, you're with me," said Bramble. He was trying to take charge as usual.

"That's not fair!" said Bracken and Berry. "Why can't Teasel come with us, Marr? Our hollow is much bigger than Bramble's."

Mellow held up her paws.

"You can all sleep together," she told Bramble, Bracken, Berry and Teasel. "Then Lop and Lilly can have Bramble's place."

Everyone agreed it was a much better idea. The four young bucks raced along a short tunnel to a cosy hollow, tucked between tree roots.

On the floor was a bed of straw and lavender. Mellow knew the smell of lavender helped rabbits to sleep.

"I'm glad that's settled," said Barley, yawning. "Now we can all go to bed!"

Lop and Lilly yawned too.

"I'm so tired," said Lop. "I could sleep on a prickly gorse bush!"

"Me too," said Lilly. "Goodnight, Mellow. Goodnight, Barley."

"Goodnight, everyone!" said Mellow.

Bramble couldn't sleep a wink for
thinking about the ghostly rabbit. He
repeated the rhyme over and over again:

"One, two, three,

Touch the rock and see,

The ghost of rabbit Rowan,

And a golden apple tree!"

Bracken, Berry and Teasel were wide
awake too.

"I wish we could find the treasure," said Bramble. "Marr says it's just a story, but I think it's true."

"We'd have to go on Windy Moor," said Bracken nervously. "It's where the scary beast lives!"

"And we'd have to see the ghost," said Berry.

"Spooky!" said Teasel.

"Well, I'm not scared," said Bramble. He wanted to show Teasel how brave he was. "Let's go on a treasure hunt."

Bracken, Berry and Teasel looked at him.

"Do you mean it?" said Bracken.

"Yes," said Bramble. "It'll be an adventure!"

Teasel wanted to help.

"I *think* I could find the way back to Windy Moor," he said.

"Good," said Bramble.

"What about the others?" said Berry.

"I'll have to tell Tansy," said Teasel. "She'll be cross if we leave her behind. Anyway, I have a feeling she knows already."

"How?" said Bramble.

"We always seem to know what the other one is thinking," said Teasel. "Even when we're apart. It's a twin thing."

"Wriggly worms!" said Bramble.

"Slugs and snails!" said Bracken.

"That's amazing," said Berry. Then, "I think Fern and Wisher would want to come too."

"Okay," said Bramble. "We'll wake them up and ask them. Don't make a noise. We don't want Marr and Parr to hear!"

To Bramble's surprise, Fern, Wisher and Tansy were still awake, whispering excitedly.

"Hello," said Fern. "What are you doing here?"

Bramble told them their plan.

"That's exactly what we're going to do!" said Tansy. She exchanged glances with Teasel.

"A voice gave me a message," said Wisher.

"We think it's about Rowan's Rock," said Fern.

"What did it say?" said Bramble. He was a bit upset. The treasure hunt had been *his* idea. He'd thought of it first!

"I would have told you sooner," said Wisher. "But I never got the chance. Things kept happening."

She repeated the words:

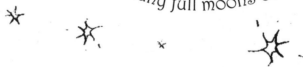

High on a hill where the wind blows cold,
There stands a rock, many full moons old.

"Hm!" said Bramble. "It doesn't say anything about treasure."

"But don't you think it's strange?" said Fern. "Wisher's message came the same day we heard about Rowan's Rock."

"It's a sign," said Tansy.

"Why are we wasting time?" said Berry. "Wisher's message is important."

"Okay," said Bramble, taking charge again. "Tansy and Teasel can show us the way to Rowan's Rock. Right?"

Everyone nodded.

"We're meant to go there," said Wisher. "I know we are."

"I'm scared," said Fern. "What if the beast . . . ?"

"I'll protect you," said Bramble. "This is our chance to find the golden apples! You heard what Marr said. She's never met a rabbit who has seen the ghost, or found the treasure. But I've got a feeling we'll be lucky tonight. Follow me!"

They crept past their sleeping parents and hurried along a narrow passageway, then up a slope and out of the burrow.

Bramble and Teasel ran ahead of the others, down to the river and across the little wooden bridge. A bright, full

moon lit their way, and a breeze rustled
the branches of trees. Bramble, Teasel,
Bracken, Berry, Fern, Wisher and Tansy
scampered through dry, fallen leaves.

Swish, Swish, Swish!

"Which way, Teasel?" said Bramble.
"We came through a tunnel,"
said Teasel.

"I know the one," said Bramble. "We call it Blinker's Tunnel. It goes under the Red Dragon's tracks."

"Race you?" said Bracken.

"No," said Wisher. "Stay together. There might be foxes, or . . ."

"The beast!" said Berry. He pulled a face and grinned.

"It's not funny!" said Wisher. "We must be careful."

"Don't worry," said Tansy. "If the beast sees Berry, he'll run for his life!"

Everyone laughed, even though they knew it was dangerous. Anything could be lying in wait and ready to pounce. But it was exciting too, and the rabbits hurried on to Blinker's Tunnel.

The Ghost on the Hill

4

The owl attacked as Bramble ran out of the tunnel. He felt the sharp stab of its beak on his neck. It stung. Bramble froze. The bird gave a screech, then was gone. The others came racing after him and gathered round.

"What happened?" said Bracken. "I heard a screech. I didn't see."

"Owl!" said Bramble, trembling with fright. "He got me here." He rubbed his sore neck.

"Does it hurt?" said Tansy.

"Much?" said Teasel.

"A bit," said Bramble. He'd had a nasty shock, but he liked all the attention he was getting.

"You were lucky he didn't carry you off," said Berry.

"You could have been eaten alive!" said Fern. "I wish we hadn't come." She thought of her cosy burrow and her parents. What if they woke and found them gone? They'd worry their whiskers off! "We'd be in trouble if Marr and Parr knew what we were doing," she said. "Remember what Marr says? Sensible rabbits have careful habits."

"You can't hunt for treasure without taking risks," said Tansy, looking at Bramble. She thought he was being very brave about the owl. "I wonder why he flew away?"

"I saw a mouse near me," said Bramble. "Maybe the owl missed the mouse and attacked me by mistake . . ."

Just then, he glimpsed the flash of a pale white wing.

"Oh no! He's coming back!" cried Bramble. "Down!"

Bramble, Bracken, Berry, Fern, Wisher, Tansy and Teasel crouched, still as stones, in the long grass.

They watched the owl circle, its wings outstretched. Suddenly, the bird dived, and a split-second later, they heard the terrified squeak of a mouse. Then silence. When Bramble dared to open his eyes he saw the owl fly away towards Oak Wood. No one twitched a whisker, until Bramble finally spoke.

"It's okay," he said. "He's gone."

"Creeping caterpillars!" said Berry.

"Bugs and beetles!" said Fern, her heart beating fast.

"I haven't been so frightened since I was chased by a fox," said Bracken.

"Let's go home," said Wisher.

"No way!" said Teasel.

"We're on a mission," said Tansy.

"We can't give up now," said Berry.

Everyone agreed their plan was daring, but they would go on.

"Great," said Bramble. He'd had a nasty fright and his neck was sore, but he wanted to find the golden apples more than anything.

Tansy and Teasel tried to remember how they'd come from the moor.

"We came through Oak Wood," said Tansy.

"And got lost," said Teasel.

Fern looked worried.

"What about the owl?" she said. "He flew into the wood."

"Owls fly anywhere," said Tansy. "We'll just have to watch out."

Bracken could see how nervous
Fern was.

"Maybe there's another way?" he said.

At that moment, the wind blew
leaves from a tree. Wisher watched them
fluttering down, until one landed on her
nose. Her ears tingled. For a reason she
couldn't explain, she pointed to a path
outside the wood.

"That will take us to Wild Moor,"
she said.

The others looked surprised.

"How do you know?" said Teasel.

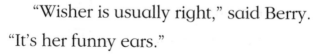

"It's just a feeling," said Wisher.

"Wisher is usually right," said Berry. "It's her funny ears."

"I wish I had ears like Wisher's," said Tansy.

Bramble didn't understand how Wisher often knew things. Her special powers were a mystery! But something told him she was right about the path.

"I'll lead the way," he said.

The rabbits set off along Wisher's path. It went along one side of Oak Wood and soon they came to a wild, grassy place.

"We're here!" cried Teasel. "This is Windy Moor!"

"Look," said Tansy, pointing to the top of a hill. "There's Rowan's Rock!"

Even from the bottom of the hill the stone rabbit looked huge. The moon shone brightly through its eyes. The giant rabbit seemed to stare down at the young rabbits who were crouched at the foot of the hill. They had never seen anything like it.

"Oooo!" they said.

"No wonder the beast in Marr's story was scared," said Bramble.

"P-p-p-please don't talk about b-b-beasts," said Bracken. "This is where the four-eyed monster lives!"

Everyone looked nervously about.

"Don't worry," said Bramble. "I'll keep an eye out for trouble. Let's go up there."

Bracken, Berry, Fern, Wisher, Tansy and Teasel followed Bramble up the hill. They hopped easily over the short grass until, suddenly, they came to a patch of mist. Bramble tried to find a way through the wisps of white.

"We have to keep going . . ." he said.

Then stopped. An animal had stepped from behind a bush. It was blocking his way.

"Baa!"

"Wha-what was that!" said the others, bumping into each other behind him.

"Is it the b-b-beast?" said Bracken.

"Is it b-b-big?" said Berry.

"Does it look f-f-fierce?" said Fern.

"Has it got sh-sharp t-t-teeth?"
said Tansy.

"F-f-four eyes?" said Teasel.

Wisher was puzzled. She was
frightened, but wondered why her ears
hadn't warned her of danger.

"Please, Bramble?" she said. "Tell us."

Just then the mist cleared and Bramble
saw the creature clearly.

"It's only a sheep!" he said.

"Baa!" said the creature and walked
away.

"Ha!" said Bramble, feeling a bit silly.
"Come on. We're nearly at the top!"

Rowan's Rock towered above them.
The ears were so tall that Bramble
thought their tops might touch the stars.

He led the rabbits around the rock, and thought about brave Rowan who'd saved her family from the beast. He remembered the rhyme that Marr had told them:

"One, two, three,
Touch the rock and see,
The ghost of rabbit Rowan,
And a golden apple tree!"

"Go on," said Bracken. "Touch the rock. We might see the ghost!"

"We dare you," said Tansy and Teasel.

"All right," said Bramble. He'd never seen a ghost and didn't know what to expect. But he supposed it couldn't be more frightening than being attacked by an owl. Bramble went up to the rock and patted it with his paw three times.

He waited. Nothing happened. Then, from behind the rock, they heard a noise.

"*Whooooo-ARRH-OOOooo!*"

Six rabbits jumped with fright. One peered around the rock and grinned.

"BERRY!" they cried.

Tansy was first to recover.

"Obviously the *real* ghost didn't hear you, Bramble," she said. "Try again. Pat the rock harder and say the words."

"Okay," said Bramble. Then to Berry, "No funny business!" He hit the rock three times saying: "One, two, three, touch the rock and see, the ghost of rabbit Rowan, and a golden apple tree!"

A sudden wind nearly blew the rabbits off their paws. It whistled round and round the rock in a rage. Then came the rain. It poured and soaked their fur. Bramble looked up and saw the moon slip behind a cloud, then everywhere was dark. The rabbits huddled together, shivering with cold and fear.

"Bugs and beetles!" said Fern. "I think we've made the ghost angry."

"Keep close to me," said Bramble. "I'm not afraid of . . ." His eyes opened wide.

Out of the gloomy darkness, a shimmering green shape appeared. It looked like a rabbit, glowing and hovering above the ground. Everyone stared. They knew without a doubt that this was Rowan's ghost.

The Treasure Tree

5

The wind and rain stopped, almost as suddenly as they had started. The moon came out from behind the cloud and shone brightly once more. The ghostly rabbit beckoned to them.

"I th-th-think it wants us to follow," said Bramble.

"G-g-go on then," said Bracken. "I'll be r-r-right b-b-behind you."

"M-m-me too," said Berry. "I'm n-n-not sc-sc-scared of a g-g-ghost."

"Well, I am," said Fern.

"So are w-w-we!" said Tansy and Teasel.

Wisher's ears were tingling again, but somehow she knew they weren't in any danger. Wisher was sure it was a good sign, and felt calm as she stared at the shimmering light.

"There's nothing to be afraid of," she said. "Rowan was a good rabbit, wasn't she? Her ghost wants to help us."

"Wisher's right," said Bramble.

He saw another chance to show
Tansy and Teasel how brave he was.

"Come on. We mustn't keep the
ghost waiting."

Bramble, Bracken, Berry, Fern,
Wisher, Tansy and Teasel ran after the
ghost rabbit, which had moved a little
way down the hill.

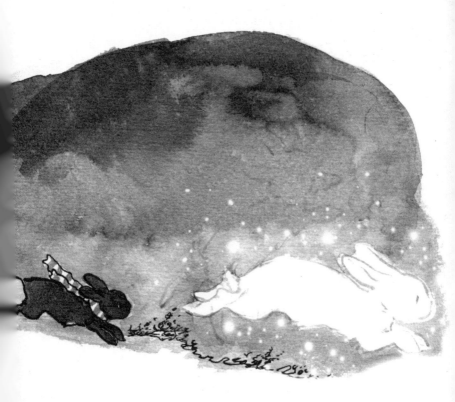

Then Bramble felt a strange thing happen. The grass seemed to melt away beneath his paws, and he drifted like a feather in the wind.

He was floating on air, chasing the dancing light across the moor, until . . . *Bump!* He landed with the others in a heap on the ground.

"Wow!" said Tansy and Teasel.

"Were we flying?" said Berry.

"It *felt* like it," said Bracken.

"Rabbits can't fly!" said Bramble, shaking his head.

"I think we just did," said Fern.

"So do I," said Wisher.

For a few minutes, everyone sat around feeling dazed.

Then they got up and looked again for the gleaming light. It was nowhere to be seen. Rowan's ghost had vanished.

"Where are we?" said Bramble.

Bracken and Wisher thought they recognised these surroundings. They were by the side of a road, near the River Ripple.

"I'm sure I've been here before . . ." said Bracken "I remember seeing a road like this when I was helping a lost rabbit called Nigel. It was the day I found a secret tunnel. You were there, Wisher. Remember?"

"That's right," said Wisher. "It was a long time ago. And there's the little wooden bridge. We're not far from home."

Bramble was disappointed.

"But where's the treasure?" he cried. "Where are the golden apples? The silly ghost has brought us here for nothing!"

He stopped. His ears pricked at a strange sound. It began as a rumble, a deep humming noise. But it quickly became a roar, and two enormous yellow eyes came rushing towards them.

The terrifying thing sped by fast and the wind flattened the rabbits' fur. The last thing they saw were two red eyes, glowing bright as fire.

"The beast!" cried Bramble, Berry and Fern.

"Blinker Badger was right," said Teasel.

Bracken and Wisher looked puzzled.

"We saw one like it when we were with Nigel," said Bracken. "Remember, Wisher?"

Wisher nodded.

"That beast had yellow eyes," she said.

"Well," said Tansy. "This one had four eyes! Red *and* yellow ones. That's much more scary!"

"It could have eaten us ALIVE!" said Fern.

Just then, Bramble spotted something
in the moonlight. It was a small tree,
just the right size for a rabbit to reach its
branches. It was full of tiny, golden apples.

"The treasure tree!" he cried. "Rowan's
ghost has brought us luck, after all."

Bramble's
Beastly
Tale
6

Bramble, Bracken, Berry, Fern, Wisher,
Tansy and Teasel sat under the tree in
the moonlight. The golden apples were
small and tasted sweet and delicious.
The rabbits were so busy eating that
they didn't notice how quickly the time
passed. Before they knew it, the sun was
beginning to rise,

"Oh no! We have to go!" said Bramble.
"We must get home before Marr and Parr
wake up."

"They'll worry their tails off if we
don't," said Bracken.

"Parr will send out a search party,"
said Berry.

"Marr will be cross," said Fern.

"Let's go," said Wisher.

"We're ready!" said Tansy and Teasel.

The rabbits dashed along the road,
then over the little wooden bridge.

From there, they scampered by the big oak and across the meadow to the burrow. Luckily Barley, Mellow, Lop and Lilly were still in bed when the young rabbits crept along the tunnel and back to their hollows. Then they all curled up and went to sleep.

A little later, Mellow came to wake them up.

"You *are* sleepy-heads today!" she said.

"Come along. It's time you were all up-burrow."

The young rabbits rubbed their eyes.

"It's too early!" said Bramble, stretching and yawning.

But Mellow shooed them outside. One by one, Bramble, Bracken, Berry, Fern, Wisher, Tansy and Teasel hopped out of the cool, dark tunnel into the morning sunshine. They joined Barley, Lop and Lilly who were under the holly bush, nibbling leaves.

"We have to go home to Burrow Bank today," Lop told Tansy and Teasel.

"The *right* way home," said Lilly. "We don't want to get lost on the moor again. We might meet the beast!"

Tansy and Teasel gave each other a look.

"Well . . ." said Teasel.

Just then, Blinker Badger came along. "What's this about the beast?" he said anxiously. "Have you seen it?"

"Yes!" said Bramble, before he could stop himself. Too late. The grown-ups were staring at him.

"WHAT!" said Barley.

"Where?" said Blinker.

"How?" said Mellow.

"Tell us," said Lop and Lilly.

Bramble didn't know how to begin.

"We wanted to find the treasure," he said. "The golden apples! We went to find Rowan's ghost . . ."

"We SAW her!" said Bracken, Berry, Fern and Wisher.

"She was green," said Tansy.

"She took us flying!" said Teasel.

The parents looked at each other.

"Hm!" said Mellow. "I expect you were all up late telling scary stories. I thought that might happen. No wonder you're all so tired. The legend of Rowan's Rock is a story. It isn't real."

"Ha! A green ghost!" said Barley.

"Flying rabbits!" said Lop.

"You'll be telling us next you found the treasure," said Lilly.

"We DID!" cried the young rabbits.

Blinker had a twinkle in his eye.

"That's marvellous!" he said. "Please, can anyone show me these lovely golden apples?"

Seven rabbits shook their heads.

"We've eaten them," said Bramble.

"Ah," said Blinker, with a smile.

"But I can show you the tree!" said Bramble.

"It's where we saw the beast with red eyes!"

"And yellow eyes," said Teasel.

"Enough!" said Mellow. "We've heard quite enough about ghosts and beasts for one day."

"But . . ." said Bramble.

"It's time for us to go," said Lop and Lilly.

They all went down to the little wooden bridge to see the Greybacks safely on their way.

Bramble, Bracken, Berry, Fern and Wisher were very sorry to say goodbye to their friends.

"We had a great time," said Tansy.

"A *real* adventure!" said Teasel.

"Come and see us again soon," said the young Longears rabbits.

"We will," said the twins.

Bramble looked for the golden apple tree, hoping to see it from the bridge. If it was there, he could prove his story. To his disappointment, it was nowhere to be seen. Mellow showed Lop and Lilly the right path along the river.

"It will take you back to Burrow Bank," she said.

"It was good to meet you, Barley," said Lop. "And you too, Blinker Badger. If it wasn't for you, we might still be lost in Oak Wood!"

The Greybacks waved and Blinker set off for home. Suddenly, Bramble remembered the owl that had attacked him near the wood. How could I have forgotten? he thought. It was the most frightening thing that's ever happened to me! His neck was still sore.

"Look, Marr. Look, Parr," he said, showing them the place where the owl had hurt him. He described what had happened.

"See? We *were* there," said Bracken.

"We saw it happen," said Berry.

"With our own eyes!" said Fern.

"It was scary," said Wisher.

Barley and Mellow looked at Bramble's neck.

There *was* a mark! Barley was confused. Bramble had told such an amazing tale he didn't know what to believe.

"If some of this *is* true," said Barley, "you were very silly to leave the burrow last night! I suppose it was Tansy and Teasel's idea? I knew they'd be up to mischief!"

"Parr is right," said Mellow. "What were you thinking? Silly rabbits have careless habits!"

"We're sorry, Marr. Sorry, Parr," said the young rabbits.

Bramble wanted to tell his story again, but Mellow took him away to see to his wound.

As she gently wiped his fur with a dock leaf, Mellow wondered how much of Bramble's story could be true. She could see he had been attacked. But what of the rest of his tale? She shook her head, unable to make much sense of it all.

"It will be better soon," she said, and gave Bramble a kiss.

That night, Bramble couldn't stop thinking about everything that had happened. If only he could find a way to make Marr and Parr believe him about Rowan's ghost and the treasure. He closed his eyes and wished . . .

A little later, when Mellow came to say goodnight, she found Bramble fast asleep. She was just tip-toeing away when she caught sight of something on the burrow floor. She bent to pick it up. It was a tiny, golden apple.

"Well I never!" said Mellow.